The Emperor's New Clothes

CARAMEL TREE

Daniel, The Emperor's Dresser

Once upon a time, there was a young man named Daniel. Daniel worked as a dresser in the Emperor's Palace.

Daniel's job was to help the Emperor choose new clothes. This was hard work because the Emperor changed his clothes every hour.

The Emperor spent all his money on buying beautiful and expensive new clothes. He never cared about his people.

2

The Magic Thread

One day, Daniel had a great idea.

"Emperor," said Daniel. "I met a magician yesterday. She gave me magic thread."

"Magic thread?" asked the Emperor. "Yes," said Daniel. "The magic thread can make the most beautiful clothes. The magician said only the wise can see those clothes."

The Emperor was excited to hear this news. He wanted to have new clothes that only the wise could see.

"You must make me new clothes with the magic thread," said the Emperor.

"I will," said Daniel, "but first I
need a work place."

"Don't worry," said the Emperor.
"I will give it to you."

The Big Room and the Large Loom

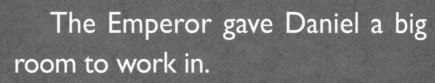

The Emperor gave Daniel a big room to work in.

"Now, make me my new clothes," demanded the Emperor.

"Yes. But now I need a loom to weave the thread," said Daniel.

"Don't worry," said the Emperor.

The Emperor ordered his servants to carry a large loom into Daniel's new room.

Daniel pretended to work on the large loom in his big room.

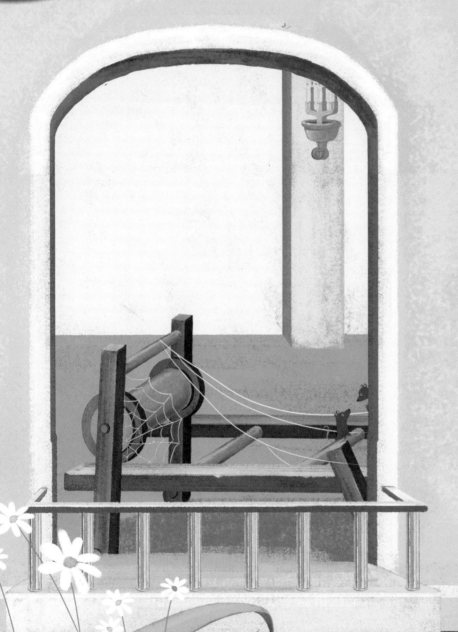

Many days passed. The Emperor called Daniel. "Are my new clothes ready?" asked the Emperor.

24

"Almost," answered Daniel. "I just need more food and drink to continue weaving."

"Don't worry," said the Emperor.

The Emperor ordered his servants to bring the best food and drink for Daniel.

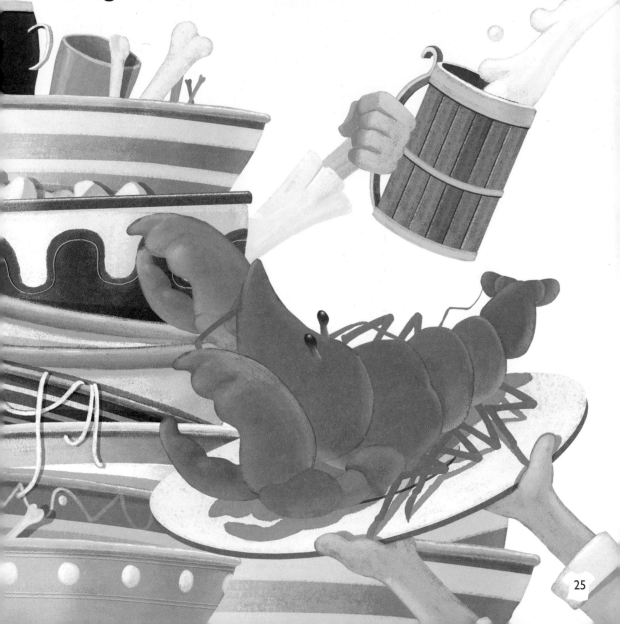

More days passed. The Emperor wanted to wear his new clothes.

"Are my new clothes ready?" asked the Emperor.

"Almost," answered Daniel. "I just need a strong white horse to go and get more magic thread."

"Don't worry," said the Emperor.

The Emperor gave Daniel a strong white horse.

Daniel went riding every day and pretended to bring back more magic thread.

Chapter 5

The New Clothes

After fifteen days, Daniel came to see the Emperor.

"Your new clothes are ready. And only the wise will see your new clothes," Daniel said.

"Where are my new clothes? Show me!" said the Emperor.

"They are right here," said Daniel. He stretched out his arms.

But the Emperor could not see anything. There was nothing in Daniel's arms.

"What is the matter? Can't you see your new clothes?" asked Daniel.

The Emperor thought carefully. Why couldn't he see the clothes? Wasn't he wise?

The Emperor finally said, "Ummm... My new clothes are beautiful."

All the servants were confused, but they also said the new clothes were beautiful. They didn't want people to think they were not wise.

The Emperor put on the new clothes that he could not see.

"Oh, yes!" said the Emperor. "These new clothes look great on me."

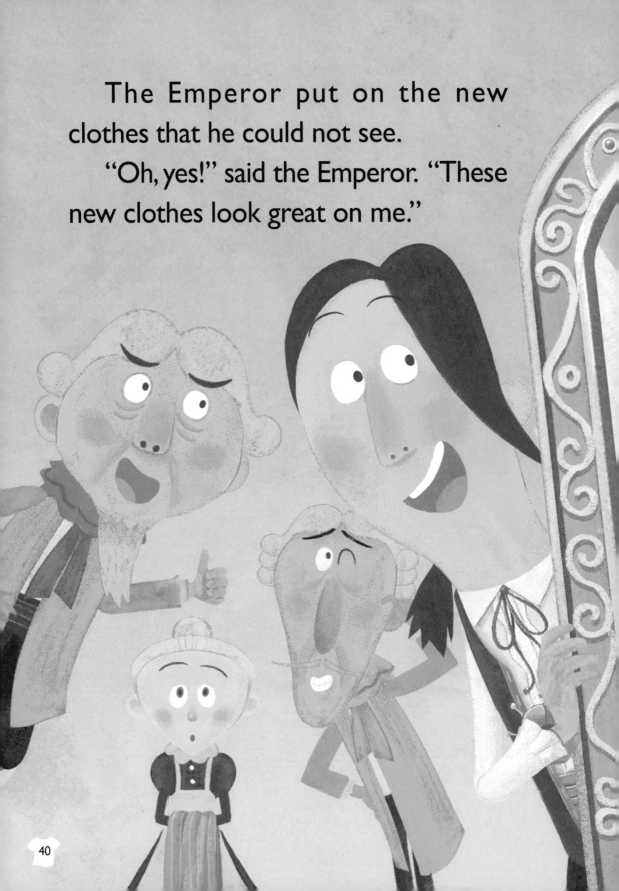

Chapter

6

Marching Through the Town

The Emperor went marching through the town to show off his new clothes.

Everyone was amazed to see the Emperor marching in his underwear. But they were too afraid to laugh or tease the Emperor.

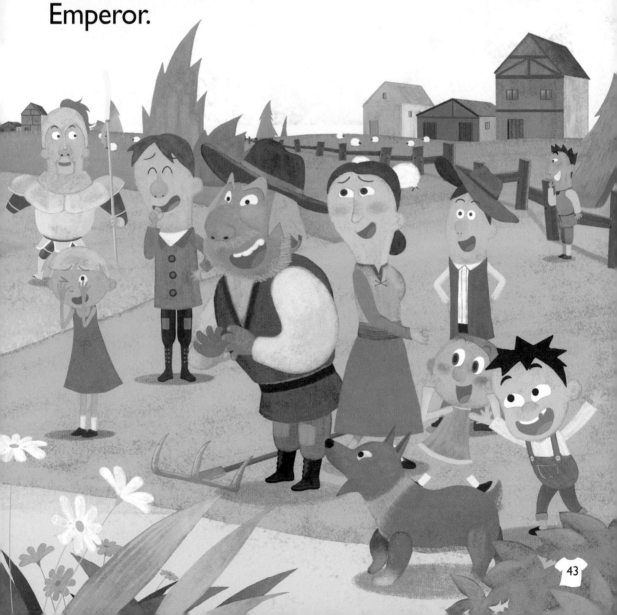

Everyone clapped hands as the Emperor walked past.

The Emperor was surprised. 'Why *can all my people see my new clothes? Are they wise, too?*' he thought.

The Emperor wished he was as wise as his people were. He wished he could see his new clothes.

After that, the Emperor stopped spending money on expensive new clothes. He realized that he was not very wise after all.

As for Daniel, he became very rich. He stayed in the best room in the Palace, ate the best food, and went horse riding every day.

All he had to do was to make sure he had new clothes for the Emperor every week.